THE PRETEND MAIL ORDER BRIDE

MAIL ORDER BRIDES OF MILES GULCH

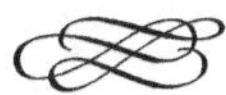

SUSANNAH CALLOWAY

Tica House Publishing

Sweet Romance that Delights and Enchants!

PERSONAL WORD FROM THE AUTHOR

Dearest Readers,

Thank you so much for choosing one of my books. I am proud to be a part of the team of writers at Tica House Publishing who work joyfully to bring you stories of hope, faith, courage, and love. Your kind words and loving readership are deeply appreciated.

I would like to personally invite you to sign up for updates and to become part of our **Exclusive Reader Club**—it's completely Free to join! We'd love to welcome you!

Much love,

Susannah Calloway

Mail Order Brides
Angel Bride
SUSANNAH CALLOWAY
AMISH RECIPE BOOKLET
Amish
with love
FIRE ON THE HIGHLANDS
OCHRAN

CONTENTS

Listening to the snores coming from the parlor downstairs, Hayley tiptoed into her room, fearing the squeak of the floorboards. Though Roger seldom woke from his drunken stupors until the following morning, there were times when he'd awaken much earlier.

If he did, Hayley would no doubt be beaten yet again.

I have to escape—this is my only chance. Another may not come for weeks, or even months.

Moving quickly, her ears fastened on the snores from below, she packed clothes, a few books, some mementos, and made certain she took every bit of jewelry her mother had left her.

"He's not going to use any of it to pay for his drinking," she muttered. "He's already gone through the family fortune."

She also made certain she packed every letter she'd received from her grandmother in Wyoming. She didn't dare leave them behind for Roger to use in tracking her down. Once she made her escape from him and his abuse, she planned to be lost in the vast expanse called Wild West.

On the bed sat her handbag. In it, she had the last bit of money left to her when her parents died. And the train ticket to Miles Gulch, Wyoming. While Roger had left the house to gamble with his friends, Hayley had taken the opportunity to empty the last bit of money from the tin can in the kitchen and the money from the bank and buy the ticket.

"Now he'll drink away only what he earns," she commented with a slight smile, her voice pitched low so it wouldn't carry.

He'll also be so angry that if I am anywhere in this town, he'll track me down and kill me.

Her heart was racing now that she had packed, for if Roger came upstairs right then he'd instantly know what she was planning, Hayley glanced around for whatever she didn't want to leave behind. Not seeing a anything, Hayley glanced at the clock. The time had come.

Carrying the heavy satchel, she crept slowly down the stairs, again listening for the sounds that Roger might be awake. The snores continued, unabated. As Hayley passed the parlor, she lowered her satchel to the floor and peered in.

Roger sat, his head thrown back, in his great chair near the fire on the hearth. The light from the blaze illuminated his once handsome profile. Hayley remembered the day she met him. He seemed so intelligent, so well respected among the people in the city, a man with a great head for business and greater prospects.

The day after her wedding, she realized she had married a beast.

In the years since, he'd gained weight, his face florid and often petulant. Like an overgrown infant, he pouted and whined, but used his fists like a boxer. Little about him attracted her now, and the sheer number of bruises and broken bones he'd given her in the years since her wedding had worn away what love she had for him.

Leaving the parlor and her husband, Hayley plucked her heavy winter cloak from the stand near the front door. Donning it, she tossed the hood over her head, then picked up her satchel. With no regrets about leaving her home in the middle of the night, she went out into the icy Pennsylvania wind.

The hansom cab that had been arranged awaited her.

Tipping his cap, the driver tossed her satchel into the back, then handed her up into its questionable shelter from the wind. "Where to, ma'am?" he asked.

Hayley gave him the address of her good friend, Rose. Rose's husband had actually paid the man to pick her up at that hour, but clearly hadn't told him where to take her. She settled into the seat, then took another long look at what had been her home.

She then turned away and stared resolutely forward as the driver cracked his whip.

"Hayley!"

Rose met her at the door to their impressive and almost palatial townhouse, giving Hayley an exuberant greeting as though they hadn't seen one another for years. "Come in, get out of that wind, you'll catch your death."

Grateful to be out of the cold, Hayley dropped the hood of her cloak. "It's certainly winter out there tonight."

"Let me take your cloak."

Rose removed the wool garment to hang on the stand, then ushered Hayley to the guest room. "William is waiting for us in the parlor. There's a lovely hot fire going as well as tea or wine, whatever you prefer."

"Warmed wine?"

Hayley left her satchel on the bed, then followed her hostess to the parlor. Rose had been her best friend since finishing school and had married a wealthy industrialist named William Carter. Hayley would stay the night, then depart for the train station early the following morning.

"Ah, there you are, Hayley," William declared warmly, rising from his chair near the fire to greet her. "Have a seat, please. How are you? Did you make your clean getaway?"

Hayley accepted a glass of wine from the Carter's butler. "I hope so. He's drunk again, and you know he'll come here first thing. He'll realize I came here."

William waved off her worry. "Let him. Rose and I will admit we let you stay the night, then you boarded a train for some unknown destination. Should he try to get rough, Harry here will toss him into the gutter. Right, Harry?"

"Of course, sir."

"Harry here was once a boxer," William confided. "I would really enjoy seeing him put Roger in his place."

Rose shook her head. "Don't fuss, Hayley, we can handle Roger if he comes here looking for you. He'll soon decide that seeking you out just isn't worth the effort."

Hayley drank from her glass, feeling its warmth spread outward from her stomach. "I hope you're right. I never want to see him again."

"The man is a brute," William said with a snort. "He doesn't deserve you. Not a lovely young lady such as yourself, Hayley."

"You're too sweet, William." Hayley smiled, for she was very fond of him, and considered Rose a very lucky woman to have married him.

"Nonsense. You're what? Twenty-three? You'll find a good man out there in the West, you mark my words, Hayley, my dear. Had I not already married my lovely Rose here, I'd have played for your hand."

"William, you're teasing me."

Hayley felt her face flush red, perhaps a mixture of the wine, the heat from the fire in addition to his compliments. In her marriage to Roger, he constantly belittled her, told her repeatedly she was ugly, and a very poor wife. Because of him, she had a scar on her left cheekbone, another over her left eye, and her honey blonde hair had strands of silver in it.

"Of course, I am," William gushed, grinning. "I am trying to cheer you up."

"Well, you are managing it," Hayley replied with a light laugh.

"Good," Rose added. "Your outlook on life has become so bleak, Hayley. You must promise me letters as often as possible. And you must find a good man to marry out there in the wild lands."

Hayley looked down at her glass. "How can I marry again, Rose? I'll still be legally married to Roger."

"Don't you worry about that." Rose reached over and patted her hand. "William here can assist you with attorneys who will help you dissolve your marriage."

In shock, Hayley lifted her head. "I never considered that."

"It's certainly not common," William replied, nodding sagely as he puffed on his pipe. "But there are laws in place now. You have a legal right to dissolve the marriage due to several factors. His drinking is one of them, the abuse is another."

"I never – thought," Hayley began slowly, "there was any hope for me in escaping him. Maybe, I don't have to leave. I don't have to go to Wyoming."

Rose held her hand up, halting her. "Escaping the marriage doesn't mean escaping *him*. If you are anywhere in this state, Hayley, he will find you. He will hurt you. As much as I'll miss you, you *must* leave."

"Rose is quite correct," William added. "You're not safe within a hundred miles of that evil man. Perhaps not even a thousand miles. Wyoming, I hear, is a wild country, and Roger is unlikely to find you in such a place. It's the last region he'll look for you."

Hayley nodded. "You're right. But still, this is my home, and he is driving me from it. I don't like it."

Rose took her hand, smiling. "Think of it as an adventure, sweetie. Your grandmother is there, so it can't be too terribly inhospitable. Think of your reunion with her."

"She and my mother had a terrible falling out," Hayley admitted. "Years ago. I'm actually surprised she invited me to come live with her."

"You're her only family," Rose pointed out. "How could she turn her back on you?"

"My mother wasn't very nice to her."

"But you are not your mother," William said sternly. "Live and let live—let bygones be bygones. You will be good for her, and she will be good for you."

"As long as Roger never finds out where I went," Hayley commented slowly. "I live in terror of that."

Shortly after dawn the next morning, Hayley kissed and hugged Rose and William on their front stoop. "Thank you so much for your friendship and hospitality," she said. "I will write as often as I may."

"God bless you," Rose told her, weeping. "I'll miss you so much."

"Not as much as I'll miss you." Hayley hugged Rose again. "Don't cry. Think of me as finally free."

Rose sniffled and wiped her face with a hankie. "I know, dear. Now go and let me have my cry. You'll miss the train."

William handed the cab driver not just Hayley's luggage, but the fare as well. Then he assisted her up into the carriage and kissed her knuckles. "We will both miss you. Be well, Hayley."

"You, too, William."

Hayley looked back as the cab started forward, gazing at her friends waving from in front of their house, and wished she could cry. Roger had all but beaten all tears from her. She waved from the window before turning to face forward. And gazed into her new future.

At the train station, a porter took her satchel while the conductor examined her ticket. "Very good, madam, your berth is just behind the dining car. Right there."

"Thank you."

Hayley walked with the other passengers to the train, and boarded. She had purchased a tiny, private berth with a narrow bed, and hot meals served on the train. She didn't use her own name when she purchased her ticket. Should Roger come to the station to seek her, he would ask for Mrs. Hayley Roxbury.

Not Miss Marlene Jones.

Finding her small quarters with her satchel already inside, Hayley sat down, and gazed out the window. Roger would be waking right about now, she thought, imagining his reaction when he found her gone. She almost smiled as she pictured his rage.

Yet, Roger in his rage was no laughing matter.

The train's piercing whistle interrupted her thoughts. Slowly at first, then gaining in speed, the train departed the station. Soon, the city passed by at an incredible pace, leaving Roger and her miseries behind forever.

Goodbye, Roger. Enjoy your life as a free and single man. Please don't look for me.

Yet, Hayley knew he would. Roger was the kind of man who refused to let go of what he thought belonged to him. And that included his wife. Still, Wyoming was a very long way from Pennsylvania, and in order to make a living, Roger had to work. Adventure trips to the wild west would not be conducive for his work schedule.

But Hayley understood obsession.

She had lived with it for five years.

CHAPTER 2

His mouth tasting as though a cat had buried its offal in it, his head thumping in a beat that matched his heart, Roger staggered from his chair. The fire had gone out, and he was cold. Why hadn't Hayley kept it going? It was one of her duties as his wife and the keeper of his home.

Rubbing his arms, shivering, he strode from the parlor. Encountering the maid who came on a daily basis to clean, but didn't live there, he demanded, "Where's my wife?"

"I haven't seen her, sir."

"Blast it all, she should be up by now. Check the kitchen."

The maid, a timid creature if there ever was one, rushed away from him. Roger knew she was terrified of him, just as Hayley was, and that knowledge made him feel superior. Women were created to serve men; he'd known that all his life. Beating them kept them in line, too afraid to rebel against his authority.

"She's not in the kitchen, sir," the maid said upon returning.

"Is she still in bed? Check, no, forget it, I'll do it myself."

Thinking of what he would do upon finding his wife still in bed at that hour, Roger slowly climbed the stairs. His aching head and nauseous belly wouldn't permit a faster pace. Yet, he felt well and able enough to black her eye, maybe both of them.

"Hayley," he roared. "Get out of that blasted bed."

He kicked her door open.

She wasn't in her room. Her bed didn't look as though it had been slept in. Rushing to her armoire, Roger jerked the door open. Most of her gowns were gone. As was the canvas satchel he knew she kept there. Swearing, he jerked open her jewelry box.

It, too, was empty.

Throwing it across the room, Roger stormed to his own chamber. Hayley had *left him*. Gone, perhaps in the night while he slept off the whiskey he'd indulged in. But she wouldn't get far. He washed, shaved and dressed in fresh clothes, mentally planning on Hayley's just punishment for daring to leave him.

"She's gone to that friend of hers, Rose," he grumbled, donning his coat. "I'll drag her back by her ear, so I will."

Without his breakfast or even his morning coffee, Roger slammed his way from his townhouse. Hailing a passing cab, he climbed in, and gave the driver Rose's and William's address. "Hurry, please."

Despite his demand, the horse, mule and oxen traffic interfered with speed. The cab's single horse managed a trot at best, leaving Roger to fume at the slow pace. Though few horses could gallop in the midst of all the wagons, buggies, carriages and riders, Roger needed that very gallop.

The cab driver halted the horse at the townhouse, a place Roger had envied for a long time. Yet, his mind refused to indulge… for he had drank his way through the wealth Hayley's parents had left her. He envied others yet found no fault in his own actions.

"Wait here," he snapped to the driver, jumping down to the curb.

Taking his walking stick, he rapped smartly on the door, and waited with little patience for it to open. When it did, he gazed at the rather large and impressive frame of the butler.

"I wish to see your master," Roger declared, pushing past the man without waiting for an invitation.

"I'll fetch him, sir."

The foyer almost daunted him in its rich furnishings, and Roger compared it to his own – a small affair that lacked much that Roger wished it had. The butler vanished down a corridor, where others branched off the foyer. Roger tried to peer down them, to see where they led.

"Roger."

Distracted by William's approach, shadowed by the big butler, Roger tried to place a pleasing mien on his face. "William. Good to see you again."

"What brings you here so early in the morning?"

William stared at him with a flat, unemotional and not very welcoming expression in his gaze. Roger almost halted, floundering, feeling pinned beneath those implacable eyes.

He remembered how influential William was in certain circles and found a bright smile.

"Ah, er, did Hayley come here?" he asked. "She is not at home, and I thought perhaps she –"

"She was here." William's hard expression didn't change. "She's gone, Roger. Took a train this morning."

Flabbergasted and shocked, Roger tried to find sense in what he'd just been told. Hayley gone from town? How could she? How *dare* she? "Uh, well, where did she go?"

"I have no idea," William replied, cold. "Stayed the night, then departed. Now if you'll excuse me –"

He started to turn. Roger grabbed his arm.

"I think you know where she went," he began, his voice tight. "And you *will* tell me."

William gazed at Roger's hand, then into his eyes. "Harry. Please escort the gentleman out."

To his dismay, Roger found his own arm gripped with a vise-like hand. Nearly lifted off his feet, he barely touched the floor with his toes as the butler half dragged him to the door. Opening it, the butler shoved him out. Flailing his arms, Roger tried to keep his balance, but toppled ignominiously down the steps.

Gathering himself, he looked up in time to see the door slammed. Cursing, Roger stood up, dusting himself off. With a final glare at the closed door, he returned to the hansom cab. "They know good and well where she went."

Climbing back in, he ordered the driver to take him home. *I'll find out where that little tart went. She can't have gone far—*

she's probably here in the city still. Too scared of her own shadow to leave.

As the driver turned the horse around, Roger stared at the townhouse, wondering if perhaps Hayley was inside. It made sense that William would *say* she left on a train. Meanwhile, Hayley, his lawful wife and his property, enjoyed their hospitality.

"I'll find her," he grumbled. "I know they are harboring her. And when I get her back…."

He left that thought unfinished. For when he found her, Hayley would sincerely regret her brief moment of independence.

"You are *mine*," he snapped under his breath. "Mine."

CHAPTER 3

Hayley stepped off the train into a blast of frigidly cold wind. Tightening her cloak around her slender frame, she shivered, observing the piled snow from a recent storm. Other passengers disembarked to stretch legs, but Hayley suspected she was the only one whose destination was this dismal place named Miles Gulch.

"Someone picking you up, Miss?"

A porter stood just behind her with her satchel.

"I believe so," she replied. "I know his name, but not what he looks like."

"Could that be him?"

Hayley looked in the direction he pointed. A man in his middle twenties with thick dark hair to his collar strode across the platform, his brilliant blue eyes fixed on her. He wore a thick wool coat, a broad brimmed cowboy hat with a gun strapped to his hip. Tales of the wild west informed her of lawless men who roamed the prairies. Now she wondered if she was safer back home after all.

"Miss Roxbury?" the man asked, his voice pleasantly mellow. He doffed his hat, the wind tumbling his hair over his brow. He had the broad shoulders and lean, muscular build of a working man, and the lines around his eyes spoke of years of squinting into the wind and sun.

"Yes, that's me. Are you Mr. Westman?"

"Yes, ma'am." His polite smile turned appreciative as he met her gaze. "Mrs. Parkland sent me to fetch you, take you to her place."

"Thank you."

"Yes, ma'am. That yours?" He pointed while raking his hair back and replacing his hat.

The porter gave him Hayley's satchel, tipped his cap and headed back to the train.

"I have a buggy over here," Mr. Westman said with a gesture. "Her place is not very far from town, but it can be a hike in cold weather."

Hayley strode across the platform beside him, liking his manner and his rugged good looks. Then she immediately quashed her attraction. Still a married woman, she shouldn't be looking at other men as attractive or as potential mates. Resolute, she vowed to not seek anyone's attention, not even this very interesting young man.

"How is my grandmother?" she asked.

"She's well," he replied. "Has a tough time getting around, so she asked me to bring you out there."

"She wrote that you look after her farm."

Mr. Westman grinned. "That's a fact. She's a real nice lady, and we enjoy helping her out."

"We?"

"My boy and me. Well, Jack, he's my nephew. His folks was killed in a flash flood a few years back. So he's like my son now."

"I'm so very sorry for your loss, Mr. Westman."

"Matt. I'm just plain Matt."

He stopped at a buggy parked at the street, a chubby black horse hitched to it. After tossing her satchel into the back, he helped her into the seat.

"I know this town ain't much to look at," he commented as he untied the reins. "It's mostly ranchers and farmers, all good-hearted folks."

"It does look rather dull," Hayley admitted. She eyed the clapboard structures, the muddy streets, the wagons and horses' hooves splashing muck with every step.

He climbed up to sit beside her. "After life in a big city back east, I reckon this is quite a change."

"It is. It'll take some getting used to."

"A pretty gal like you won't be a stranger for long."

Hayley caught his appreciative glance again as Matt slapped the reins on the horse's rump. "Are there a shortage of pretty ladies in town?" she dared ask.

"Oh, yes, ma'am," he replied with a chuckle. "This here is a frontier town. Most men are single, looking for wives. A few have found women to marry through the Mail Order Bride system."

"What is the Mail Order Bride system?"

Matt eyed her with confusion. "You've never heard of it?"

"No, I'm afraid not."

"There's an agency that matches single women from back east to men in the west needing wives. As pretty as you are, I thought maybe you came west looking for a husband."

Hayley looked away from him. *He would be shocked to know I'm married and running away from an abusive man.* "I'm not looking for a husband. Not right now."

She spoke the truth anyway. Not all of it, true, yet she didn't know this man to confide in him the real reason she had come to this cold Wyoming mud hole. "Do you have a farm of your own?"

"A ranch. A couple thousand acres over yonder." He pointed to the north. "Seven hundred head of cattle, a nice little remuda."

"I'm not familiar with the term," she said, feeling out of her element.

"Oh. A horse herd, working cow horses."

The trotting horse took them through town, hooves splashing through the mud. Hayley observed the people hurrying to get in out of the wind and cold, and very few of them were women. She saw cowboys on tall horses with guns at their hips and lariats tied to their saddles, men in frock coats on the sidewalks avoiding the muck.

Narrower streets branched off the main road leading to residences. They weren't the townhouses she was familiar with, but one and two-story homes with yards. She saw no children, but she felt certain they had passed a single room schoolhouse.

"How do you find time to help my grandmother and run a ranch?" Hayley asked.

"Aww, it's not difficult," Matt replied with an easy smile. "Mrs. Parkland's place ain't far from mine, and Jack rides over every day to feed her stock."

"That is very kind of you both."

"A nice lady, your grandmother," he commented. "Jack and me both think the world of her. Is that why you came? To help her out?"

"That's part of it."

Hayley waited for the questions to follow, but they never came. Grateful for his lack of curiosity, she studied the vast prairie outside of town, the yellow grass peeking up from the snow. In the distance, animals moved, big brown lumps against the white snow.

"Are those your cattle?" she asked.

Matt glanced at them. "Buffalo. Some still roam around here, feeding the local Indians. White folks hunt them for their meat and hides like the Indians do."

"Are there many Indians around here?" she asked, now worried she'd be killed and scalped by the fierce natives.

"Some," Matt replied. "There's a Cheyenne village a few miles from here. They come into town now and then to trade."

"So they're peaceful?"

"Sure, they are." He glanced at her with amusement. "Friendly folk who don't want trouble any more than we do."

Having heard about Indian uprisings from the newspapers, Hayley wasn't certain the local tribes would stay peaceful. Matt's gesture of pointing past the horse's ears took her attention off Indians and uprisings.

"That's your grandmother's place."

The road they traveled passed a respectably large home built of stone and wood, a broad front porch wrapping at least the two sides Hayley saw. A barn stood across the wide yard complete with a corral for horses and cows, a sty with a few pigs in it. Chickens scratched and pecked in the yard, and as Matt guided the horse into it, they fled squawking. A young boy emerged from the barn. Like Matt, he wore a heavy coat.

"Whoa." Matt reined the horse in at the porch even as a woman with a thick shawl over her shoulders stepped from the house.

It had been years since Hayley had last seen her grandmother, Eunice Parkland. Though clearly much older with deeper lines in her already creased face, Eunice still bore herself with a straight back and a direct gaze.

"Hayley," she called, using a cane to walk with. "Come here, come here, Matt, you, too. Get inside out of this dreadful wind."

Hayley didn't wait for Matt's assistance in getting out of the buggy. Her emotions threatening to burst over like a river flooding a dam, she hiked her skirts and ran up the porch steps.

"Granny," she cried, enfolding Eunice into her arms. "Oh, Granny."

Eunice chuckled, patting Hayley's shoulders. "Hayley, you're finally here. I have missed you so."

Her throat tight, Hayley swallowed, trying to laugh. "I missed you, too. How are you?" Holding Eunice at arm's length, she looked her up and down. "You look great."

"I'm old, dear, just old." Eunice turned away and thumped toward the door. "It's warm in the house, and I have tea brewing. Matt, tell Jack to come inside and get warm. That boy works too hard."

Hayley half turned, finding Matt had followed with her satchel. The house was indeed warm with the fire blazing on the huge hearth in the central room. Eunice plodded toward the kitchen as Hayley looked around the comfortable house. Well furnished, it held a welcoming ambiance to it that made Hayley feel at home.

"Where do you want this, Mrs. Parkland?" Matt asked, indicating the satchel.

"In that room right there, thank you, Matt. You and Jack will stay to supper. Don't bother to argue."

Hayley had to smile at the firm order in Eunice's voice. She remembered it from her days as a child when there was no strife within her family. Removing her cloak, she hung it on a peg near the door as Matt took her satchel into what was now her room. He reappeared a moment later.

"I'm headed out for chores," Matt called toward the kitchen.

"Thank you, dear."

As he smiled at Hayley, passing her, Hayley was struck once more by how good looking he was. A generous and kind nature, she thought, comparing him to her ruthless and brutal husband. *There is no comparison.* Entering the kitchen, Hayley breathed in the scents of frying chicken.

"Thank you for letting me come, Granny."

Eunice half turned from the stove with a snort. "I certainly couldn't say no, child. Not with that brute hurting you. I told your mother he was no good, I saw that right off. But she didn't see that, nor did your father." Eunice fixed Hayley with a stern eye. "Nor did you."

"I didn't. I loved him, thought him handsome and kind. I certainly learned better."

"Now, Matt out there." Eunice went back to slicing potatoes. "Fine young man. Would make you a wonderful husband. You should think about that."

"Granny." Hayley sat at the table, folding her hands in her lap. "I'm still married. I didn't tell Matt my circumstances, and I'd appreciate it if you didn't tell him either. It's family business."

"I won't tell him anything, child," Eunice retorted. "You have to get that brute out of your life. Time to move on."

"William said he will get my marriage dissolved."

"He's your friend's husband, right? What an excellent notion. Roger beating you is a far worse sin than a divorce is."

Relief brought Hayley's spirits up. "I'm glad you feel that way. Too many folks think that marriage is for life no matter what happens. That women need to make the best of it."

"My generation certainly thinks that way," Eunice agreed. "But times change. This is one of them. Perhaps the law will one day take a dim view of a man beating his wife."

"That will never happen," Hayley replied. "Wives are property, nothing more."

"How cynical you've become, dear. I hope that's something else that can change. You're much too young for such."

Hayley didn't agree, but she wouldn't be rude and contradict her grandmother. "Roger won't find me out here, will he?"

"I doubt he can get his head out of the bottle long enough to realize you're gone."

"I'm terrified he will, Granny," Hayley said, thinking of Roger's blind rages. "If he finds out where I am, he *will* come here. I'm scared you will get hurt."

Eunice didn't bother to turn around. "If that fool steps one foot onto my property, he'll meet the business end of my shotgun."

CHAPTER 4

"You got that cow milked, son?"

Matt pumped water into the trough for the horses and cows, observing Jack herd the chickens into the barn to keep them safe through the coming night.

"Yessir."

"Did you scatter feed for those birds?"

"Yessir. The cats haven't gotten their milk yet, though."

Shutting down the pump, Matt went into the barn to the pail of foaming milk and dumped a portion of it into a pan for the mewing cats. They, too, would spend the long and cold winter night shut inside the barn where they'd sleep in the straw. The cats and the chickens shared the barn with Mrs. Parkland's elderly saddle-horse, the milk cow, and her half-grown calf.

Taking the rest of the milk outside, Matt set the pail on the ground, and with Jack's help, shut the barn doors.

"We've been invited to supper," he said as they crossed the yard against the howling wind.

"That pretty lady is really her granddaughter?" Jack asked.

"Sure is."

"From back east?"

"Pennsylvania."

Matt recalled the moment he first saw Miss Roxbury standing on the platform. In awe of her elegant beauty and bearing, he half wondered if all back east women were as poised and aloof as she. True, she seemed quite reserved where the reservations had long been rubbed off Mrs. Parkland. And he absently wondered what Miss Roxbury might be like with her guard down.

Inside the house, both he and Jack removed coats, hats and boots, scenting the hot food emanating from the kitchen. Hunger gnawed at his belly. Mrs. Parkland's cooking was much better than his own, and he didn't mind her paying him for his work with food and mothering. His parents were gone even as Jack's were, so he appreciated Mrs. Parkland's tendency to fuss over them both.

"Come in here, you two," Mrs. Parkland ordered from the kitchen. "There's hot tea to warm you."

Miss Roxbury gave him a wary smile as he entered the kitchen, then her eyes fell to Jack. Matt dropped his hand to Jack's shoulder. "Uh, this is Jack. Jack, this is Miss Roxbury."

"Please," she said in that accent Matt found fascinating, "call me Hayley. I don't think we need to be so formal."

"How do you do, ma'am," Jack asked politely.

"Very well, thank you. Let me pour you gentleman some tea."

Matt and Jack sat obediently at the table as Hayley brought them mugs, then returned to the stove for the pot. Her graceful movements and eastern formality appealed to Matt. Though she didn't smile much, he strongly suspected that once someone got past her reserve, she had a beautiful smile.

"How was the trip from Pennsylvania?" Matt asked as Hayley poured tea into their mugs.

"Very long," she replied, her large hazel eyes glinting with a humor her mouth didn't reflect. "Tiring, but to cross half the country and seeing so much beauty was almost worth it."

"Hayley is my only living kin," Mrs. Parkland commented from the stove. "It's right that she come out here. The city is no good for one's health."

"What's a big city like, ma'am?" Jack asked, blowing on his tea.

"Noisy," Hayley replied, opening a cabinet door to start setting the table. "Crowded. But it has restaurants, and opera houses, and theaters. Many things to do and see in the city."

"Not much to do way out here," Matt said. "Except you can ride for miles and miles and never see another person. Do you ride, Hayley?"

"No, I'm afraid not. If you need to get from one place to another, you pay a cab to take you."

Matt and Jack exchanged a long, confused look. "A cab? What's that?"

"A driver with a hansom carriage," Hayley replied, her expression amused. "Most people don't have their own horses. If you can't afford a hansom cab, you walk. If you're wealthy, you might have your own horse and buggy, but even then, it's far easier to simply hail a cab."

"How odd to not have horses." Matt couldn't fathom hiring someone to take him from one place to another. "Not very practical out here."

"No, it probably isn't out here," Hayley admitted. "I expect that if I'm going to make Wyoming my home, I should learn to ride."

"I can teach you," Jack said eagerly.

"Do you have a gentle horse?" she asked, a half smile playing around her mouth. "I would like not to be bucked off."

"Oh, yes, ma'am," Jack replied. "Our old Red is as quiet as can be. Never bucked in his life."

Matt laughed. "He's a bit old for such shenanigans these days. In his younger years, he jumped around a bit."

"I could never hope to stay on when a horse jumps around," Hayley commented.

"I have a nice quiet gelding out there you can have, Hayley," Mrs. Parkland said as she crossed the kitchen with a bowl of boiled potatoes. "Well mannered and saddle wise. I will never sit a horse again."

"Granny, I didn't come to take your animals from you," Hayley protested.

"Nonsense. Out west in the territories, you need a good horse."

Dinner warmed Matt through and through, filling him with the delicious chicken, potatoes, hot bread, peas and squash. Nor could he get enough of looking at Hayley. Once or twice, he caught her looking at him when she thought he couldn't see.

Could she possibly be interested in me? She said she wasn't looking to marry, but that could change.

"While I don't want to push you boys out the door," Mrs. Parkland said at the end of the meal, "you have your own chores. And it's dark outside."

Matt didn't want to leave, as he was enjoying Hayley's company far too much. But Mrs. Parkland was right. He and Jack had to get home to the ranch and feed his hungry horses and chickens. "Thank you for the dinner, ma'am," he said, rising. "Hayley, it's been great to meet you. I look forward to seeing you again."

For a moment, he thought she'd grant him a full smile. Instead, she nodded gravely with only a tiny smile for him. "And you as well, Matt. You, too, Jack."

"Good night, Mrs. Parkland," Jack said with a grin. "See you tomorrow. Good night, ma'am."

Hayley came closer to a full smile. "Good night, Jack. Travel home safely."

"Oh, we will. There ain't no bears or wolves out there. Just coyotes."

Hayley looked mystified as Matt sent her a grin, then he and Jack headed for their coats and the front door. Turning, Matt saw Hayley standing in the kitchen entryway. She gave him a small wave. Then she went back inside.

~

The next morning, a storm blew in and snow fell in a thick burst. Matt gazed out the kitchen window at the sight, drinking his coffee. He had planned to ride out and check the cattle, but with the current storm, he thought better of it. Jack stumbled into the room, yawning enormously, and fell into a kitchen chair.

"It's snowing," he said around another mighty yawn.

"Yep. I reckon we're not riding out to check the cattle," Matt replied, turning his attention back to the storm. "We'll do our chores, then ride over to Mrs. Parkland's and feed her stock."

"I like Hayley."

Matt smiled into his coffee. "I do, too."

"Are you going to marry her?"

Almost choking, Matt replied. "That's rather sudden, isn't it? We just met her yesterday."

"But she's so pretty." Jack fought another yawn.

"Have some coffee. Then maybe you'll wake up."

Jack slumped to the coffee pot and poured himself a small cup of the black brew. He usually didn't like it but would have a cup now and again. Especially on cold mornings. "No one in town is as pretty as she is."

"I know. But sometimes being beautiful ain't enough," Matt answered, watching the snow fall. "Other things are just as important."

"Like being beautiful on the inside?"

"Exactly. We don't know her well enough to understand what's in her heart."

Jack slurped, making Matt turn and scowl.

"Sorry," Jack muttered.

"You have manners in there somewhere. Use them."

"I'll bet she's just as pretty in her heart as she is on the outside," Jack observed.

"She does seem that way," Matt agreed.

"Will you ask her to the town dance?"

"There aren't any dances until spring."

"Oh. Then how can you court her?"

Mat laughed, turning. "What makes you so sure I want to?"

"I saw the way you looked at her." Jack put his elbow on the table, his cheek on his fist. "And you need a wife."

"I do?"

"Yeah."

"Let's just say I'll see what happens with Hayley. You're right, I do like her. But I also need to know that she'll make a good wife."

"What makes a good wife?"

Matt sighed, wondering if this was a good conversation to have with a twelve-year-old. "I suppose first thing is if we love each other. Then to know if she wants children, and whether she'll cook, clean, tend the garden, help with chores. Things like that."

Jack shook his head. "That's a lot to decide on a good wife."

"And it's not an easy thing to do."

Drinking his coffee, Jack gazed blankly into space. "When will I find a wife?"

"Not for a very long time. Now let's get some breakfast before we have to deal with the weather."

After a quick meal of bacon, eggs and bread, Matt and Jack ventured into the snow to care for their stock. Jack sat on the three-legged stool to milk their cow, their barn cats waiting in a half circle with their tails twitching. Matt fed the cows and horses in the corral as well as the horses in the barn, and then broke the ice in the water trough.

He scattered feed in the barn for the chickens, gathered eggs, then threw feed in for the pigs at the furthest end of the barn. While Jack trudged through the snow to put the pail of milk in the house, Matt saddled their horses. Leaving them to continue to eat for a time, he closed the barn door, and returned to the house.

"Hayley may do us out of a job," he commented, warming himself by the stove with another cup of coffee. "We may get there only to find she took care of things."

"I don't think she knows how yet," Jack commented, washing their breakfast dishes.

"You may be right."

"She came here to take care of Mrs. Parkland. We should teach her how."

"But then we'd have no reason to go over there and get to know her." Matt grinned at Jack's stricken expression.

Huddling in their heavy coats, their hands holding hats to their heads in the strong wind-blown snow, Matt and Jack rode to Mrs. Parkland's property. Part of the road dipped through a ravine amidst a thick copse of trees that lined either side of it. The wind eased a fraction as they rode amid the tall trunks.

"What's that?"

Jack reined in his horse to point. Matt also halted, staring through the falling snow to see what Jack obviously saw. "I don't see anything."

"I think it's something dead."

Before Matt could stop him, Jack slipped down from his saddle to trot under the trees.

"If it's dead, leave it be," Matt called to him. "Mrs. Parkland's critters need us more than some dead thing."

Matt heard a sound that haunted his dreams for months after. The sharp crack of a steel trap and Jack's scream of agony.

CHAPTER 5

"Back home, all this snow would turn into slop," Hayley commented as she gazed out the window at the pristine whiteness that covered the yard and the barn's roof. "Wagons and buggies would mix the snow into the manure in the streets."

"I lived in the city once," Eunice replied from the table. "I remember the nastiness very well, thank you."

"It's rather nice to enjoy snow for its own sake," Hayley went on. "Warm and safe inside a snug home."

"With plenty of wood for a fire, I quite agree."

After the long journey on the train, Hayley had slept like one dead to the world. She had yet to unpack her clothes to hang in the armoire and wore the gown she had on yesterday. Still, she felt refreshed after sleeping on a bed that didn't rock back and forth.

Movement at the road caught her attention. Two riders galloped through the storm, heedless of any ice under the snow. Alarmed, Hayley watched as they charged toward the house. "Something's wrong."

"What?"

"I think that's Matt and Jack, but they're riding fast."

Running out of the kitchen, Hayley hiked her skirts as she crossed the sitting room rushing past the fire on the hearth. Throwing open the door, letting in a blast of icy wind and snow, she ran onto the porch.

Matt reined in, his horse's rear quarters slithering through the snow to halt in front of the porch. Jack slumped in his saddle, and only then did Hayley realize Matt held the reins to Jack's horse.

"What happened?" she cried.

Matt didn't answer immediately. Leaping from his saddle, he strode behind his mount, and pulled Jack into his arms. Leaving the horses to stand in the storm, he carried the boy into the house. "He stepped into a hunter's trap," he explained, his voice terse.

"Bring him in here," Eunice ordered crisply. "Hayley, shut that door. Then boil water, there are bandages in the cupboard to the left of the sink."

Both Hayley and Matt did as they were told. Hayley ran back to the kitchen as Matt carried Jack into one of the bedrooms. Pumping water into a kettle, she set it on the stove to heat, then found the bandages Eunice demanded.

Taking them into the bedroom, she found Jack lying on the bed with his face pale. But he seemed composed as Matt, Eunice watching, gently worked the boot off his foot. Joining them, Hayley gazed down at the ripped skin of Jack's ankle.

The ankle was highly swollen and had already turned a deep blue. Blood had crusted all around his foot.

"Move aside," Eunice ordered. "Get me a chair, please."

Obeying, Matt dragged a chair from the far side of the room. Eunice sat beside the bed, her hands on Jack's ankle.

"Do we need a doctor?" he asked, his voice ragged, hoarse.

Eunice didn't answer. Fascinated, worried, Hayley looked from Jack's face to Eunice as her grandmother gently flexed his foot, his ankle and his knee. Jack himself winced in pain, but neither cried nor begged her to stop. Eunice's hands probed the bruised and broken flesh, then stopped.

"No, there's no need to get the doctor," she said. "His ankle isn't broken. If the trap had teeth, then we'd be looking at more serious damage."

"No, the trap didn't have teeth," Matt said, clearly relieved by the diagnosis.

"Hayley, the hot water, please."

"Right."

Rushing from the room, Hayley took the kettle of steaming water from the stove and poured it into a small basin. Adding a clean cloth, she took the basin into the bedroom. Holding it where Eunice could reach it, she watched raptly as Eunice expertly washed Jack's injured ankle, then bound it with the bandages.

His foot bound tightly, Jack's pain seemed to ease, as some of the tension left his face. "It feels better," he admitted.

"Well, then, you better relax and get used to being here," Eunice told him. "You're not going anywhere for a while."

"But…" Matt stammered, "he can go home with me."

Eunice fixed him with a hard look. "He stays here where we can look after him. Hayley, there's a brown bottle of laudanum in the same cupboard. Please fetch it."

Without arguing, Hayley once more went to the kitchen and found the bottle. She seized a glass, filled it with water, grabbed a spoon, and took all back to the bedroom. Eunice accepted the bottle and the spoon with a nod, then poured a small amount of the laudanum into the spoon.

"Take this," she said, her tone not something Hayley would argue with.

Jack took the laudanum with a grimace, then hastily drank the water. "That's nasty," he declared with a shudder.

"Just so you won't like to take it," Eunice replied. "Matt, remove his other boot and make him comfortable. He'll sleep now."

Stiffly, Eunice rose from her chair, and tottered out of the room. Hayley gathered the basin of water, the laudanum and the glass, then left Matt to care for Jack. Putting the items away, she saw Eunice seated in a chair near the hearth. She looked old and careworn to Hayley, and frail.

Matt emerged from the bedroom, closing the door behind him. "I'd best take care of the stock now."

"I'll help you," Hayley said quickly. "I imagine it's a great deal of work for one person."

Matt eyed her in surprise. "You don't have to."

"I know."

Suspecting the shoes she wore were not suitable for snow and working in a barn, yet having no alternative, Hayley donned her thick cloak, and led the way into the storm. Matt led both horses by their reins, following her. The wind snapped her hair from her pins, the blonde mass whirling around her face. Holding it back as best she could, she swung open the barn's door.

Greeted by whinnies and moos from the stock, Hayley gazed around the tidy barn. It scented of animals and manure, hay and the fainter odor of molasses. Something brushed against her skirts, and in looking down, she saw a few cats rubbing their heads on her, their backs arched.

Matt led the saddled horses inside and put them in an empty stall. He took their bridles off to hang on the saddle horns, and loosened cinches. Hayley struggled to close the heavy barn door with the wind threatening to pull it from her grip.

"I'll milk the cow," Matt said, leaving the stall. "I reckon I can just tell you what to do, right?"

Hayley nodded faintly, slightly overwhelmed at the expectant eyes looking at her. She'd never been in a barn, nor fed an animal in her life. "Uh, what do they eat?"

Matt chuckled, rubbing the ears of a horse with its head hanging over the stall door. "You really are a city girl."

"Born and raised," she replied, cautiously holding her hand out for the horse to sniff. "I've never touched a horse before."

"Never?"

"Well, they pull the carriages and wagons," Hayley went on, embarrassed. "I never thought of them beyond the conveyance."

"You sure have a lot to learn about living in the west," Matt said.

Hayley thought he mocked her, but then saw his gentle, sweet smile and the warmth in his blue eyes.

"Yes, I expect I do."

"That hay over there?" Matt said, pointing. "Toss a bunch of that into those mangers. This lil lady here needs to get milked before her udders burst."

As Matt directed her, Hayley gathered loose hay into her arms, thinking she would need to wear an old dress if she was to begin barn work. The cows and the horses grabbed hay from her arms before she could toss it into the mangers. Brushing stems from her cloak and gown, she eyed Matt milking the cow, cats waiting expectantly.

"They work for their milk?" she asked, amused.

"Sure do. If they weren't here, the rats and mice would overrun this place."

Under Matt's instructions, she scattered grain for the chickens, scooped more for the horses and the cows. The outside animals had hay waiting for them there, but Matt would help her feed them. The cow milked, he poured some of it into a pan for the eager cats. His and Jack's horses received buckets of water, the other buckets refilled.

He set the pail in the snow and helped her close the massive barn door.

"We'll have to break the ice on the water trough," he hollered over the wind.

Not liking being outside in such weather, Hayley nonetheless assisted him in feeding the animals in the corral as well as the pigs in their pen. Her hair whipped around her face like a cloud, forcing her to make a mental note to tie it into a tail the next time she ventured outside.

Her feet numb, her hands hurting from the intense cold, Hayley trudged through the snow rapidly piling up on the ground. Matt's hand on her arm prevented her from slipping on the ice under the snow. Feeling certain she'd not survive living in Wyoming, she stumbled into the warmth of the house.

"Heavens, child, get out of those wet things before you get sick." Eunice sat near the fire, her heavy shawl around her shoulders. A batch of knitting sat in her lap with her gnarled hands on the needles. "I'll make some tea, there's hot water on the stove."

Eunice rose stiffly from her chair, and, using her stick, tapped her way into the kitchen.

Shivering violently, Hayley almost couldn't get her hands to work to pull her cloak and shoes off. Matt hung her cloak on the peg beside his coat, then urged her to sit beside the fire.

"I'll fetch a towel for your hair," he said.

Her lengths of hair dripped icy water onto her shoulders and bodice as the snow in it melted rapidly in the heat. Too cold to do more than rub her arms, Hayley tried to ignore the wet. Then Matt returned with a thick towel and used it to rub excess water from her hair. Though it was almost too personal for a man, a near stranger at that, to sop her dripping lengths, Hayley felt too cold to care.

"Thank you," she stammered through chattering teeth. "The rest will just have to dry."

"At least you won't have it making your dress wet," he replied with a smile, then sat near her.

Eunice returned with mugs of steaming tea. "Drink that down now, it'll help warm you."

Her hands wrapped around the hot mug, Hayley gratefully drank the hot tea, scalding her tongue, but feeling the warmth spread to her chilled bones. "I hope I can get used to being out in that weather," she murmured, her shivers abating a little.

"That'll take some time," Matt commented. "You can live here all your life and still not get used to it."

"What a comforting thought."

"At least it quits snowing in summer," he said with a laugh. "Then you can get used to the heat."

"That I can deal with."

Her tea gone, and finally warm, Hayley stood up. Eunice had fallen into a doze in her chair, her hands clasped over her knitting. With her hands, Hayley informed Matt she was going to change, and observed his quick nod of reply.

In her room, she pulled a clean gown and fresh stockings from her satchel. After she changed out of her soiled, damp dress, she spent some time unpacking her things and hanging her gowns in the armoire. Her mother's valuable jewelry – Hayley stared at the rings, the diamond necklaces and earrings. It was the last of her family's moderate fortune.

"Roger would come west for this alone," she murmured. "Even if he didn't want me."

Absently thinking of Roger, hoping he would never find her, Hayley left her room to check on Jack. The boy slept under a mound of quilts, his color good with his breathing low and even. Feeling that he'd recover just fine from his injury, she returned to the hearth fire.

"How is he?" Matt asked, his voice low since Eunice still dozed.

"Sleeping comfortably."

Picking up Matt's mug as well as her own, Hayley planned to refill them with fresh tea. Matt's fingers slowly and deliberately brushed against hers. Startled, but somehow not offended, Hayley gazed into his brilliant blue eyes. Something, she wasn't sure what, passed between them as though a spark from the fire crossed from him to her.

Could that spark light a fire between us?

CHAPTER 6

"We have no further use for your services."

An icy chill spread through Roger. "What?"

Charles, the owner of the finance and investment company where Roger worked as a manager, stared at him from across his vast teak desk. "Your employment with us is terminated, Roger."

Both baffled and stunned, Roger floundered for a moment, his mouth opening and closing stupidly. At last, he found a single word.

"Why?"

"I shouldn't have to point this out to you, as you know perfectly well how much you drink. Your work is sub-level. Your reputation is reflecting poorly on this company."

"I don't drink at work!"

Charles's eyes hardened. "Do you deny arriving for work late and hungover? That you frequently rage and curse at the other employees? That your own wife left you due to your drinking habits and the abuse you put her through?"

"How do you know about that?" Roger demanded.

Charles merely smiled without warmth. He pushed a check across the desk toward Roger. "Your pay with extra in lieu of notice of termination."

"Is William behind this?"

"Who?"

Roger studied Charles's blank expression, suspecting William was indeed whispering in Charles's ear behind Roger's back. "He is, isn't he?"

"No one is behind this except me," Charles answered. "Pack up your desk, Roger. Good-bye."

His rage threatening to overflow, creating a powerful desire to reach across the desk and strangle the man in the chair, Roger stood. Attacking a man like Charles would result in Roger being arrested. Like William, Charles had many friends across the city, scattering influence and favors like confetti. Roger himself had only gambling and drinking buddies.

Without a word, he picked up the check, folded it, and put it in his pocket. Leaving the office, he made eye contact with no one, but he was sorely conscious of the stares and the murmured voices. At his own work desk, Roger gathered his few personal possessions. He had little enough to collect, and the items went into his pockets.

He donned his heavy coat, then again without meeting anyone's eyes, he departed the place he'd worked for five years. Leaving the building, he hunched his shoulders against the biting wind. Though he knew he should consider trying to find other employment, his thoughts moved to Hayley and where she might have gone.

All his searching over the past weeks had yielded nothing. If anyone outside of William and Rose knew where she was, they refused to tell him. Hayley had no family left save her grandmother, and Roger didn't know where the old woman was. For all he knew, she had also died, leaving Haley alone in the world.

Entering the shelter of the bank, Roger stomped snow from his boots, and blew on his fingers in a vain effort to warm them. The bank teller he approached smiled professionally.

"How can I help you, sir?"

Fumbling for his check, Roger pushed it across to the man. "I need to deposit that."

He gave his account information for the teller to look up in his files. The teller returned a few moments later.

"I'm sorry, sir, that account is closed."

Roger glowered. "How can that be? I didn't close it."

"No, sir, this says it was closed by Mrs. Roger Roxbury."

Hayley closed the account. Emptied it? Took the money and left me with nothing. I'll kill her for that. Roger drew deep breaths to calm his rage, the teller watching him warily. At last, when he felt he could speak without screaming, he asked, "May I then cash this?"

"Of course."

The teller took his check, then opened his drawer with a key. He counted out Roger's pay on the counter. "You can also open another account if you wish."

"No."

Stuffing the cash into his pocket, Roger left the bank, still seething with controlled rage. How had she managed to close their account? Wasn't that up to him? Did she bat her lashes at some stupid teller? He would find her. Wherever she was, he would find her, and then she would pay for this humiliation. She owed him the jewels she took, they were his property, after all. Just as she was. Hayley would feel the pain of his wrath and beg to come home with him.

But how could he go about finding her?

Two days later on a fairly warm afternoon for winter in Pennsylvania, Roger loitered near the Carter's expansive and luxurious townhouse. He had spent time with the clerk at the train station, going over records of passengers who departed the city in recent weeks.

Hayley's name was not among them.

Roger concluded that either she never took a train at all as William had said, or she used an alias. Either way, he still had no way of finding where she went. But William and Rose Carter knew where she had gone. If they wouldn't tell him directly, he would find a different way.

He leaned against a brick wall for hours, watching the house, waiting for one of the servants to emerge. He knew the big butler couldn't be bribed for information, but one of the maids might be. Thus, he hoped that on a rather pleasant afternoon, Rose would send one or two on errands.

Sure enough, a maid in black and white attire with a lace cap on her head, a wool cloak over her shoulders, left the house. Roger pulled a ten-dollar bill from his pocket, then followed her. Ten dollars was more than the girl earned in a month, and would no doubt attract her interest.

"Excuse me," he called, trotting to catch up to her.

The maid turned, clearly surprised at being hailed. "Yes, sir?"

Roger made certain she saw the cash. "I need your help, miss," he said, keeping a charming smile on his face, his voice light and pleasant.

"What with?"

"You see, my wife left," he explained, observing that the girl didn't appear particularly intelligent and that her eyes were on the bill in his fingers. "I really want to find her, to beg her to come back to me. I love her very much, you know."

The girl frowned. "I don't know how I can help."

"Your mistress knows where she is," Roger went on. "But through a misguided sense of loyalty, she won't tell me where Hayley went."

"That's your wife?"

"Yes, Hayley Roxbury." Roger held up the bill. "This is yours, right now, if you can find out for me."

"How?"

Growing impatient, Roger worked to contain it, for if he frightened her, money or no money, she would flee. "Perhaps a letter with Hayley's return address?" he suggested gently.

"Maybe get your mistress to talk about her? Anything at all will help me. I'd be most grateful."

The maid nodded. "I can do that."

"Thank you." Roger pressed the money into her hand. "I'm Roger Roxbury, and you can get word to me at my home." He made her memorize his address. "Please, miss, I truly love my wife. I need to tell her that, but I cannot unless I know where she is."

Tucking the cash away into a pocket, the girl gave him a tentative smile. "I'll find out for you, Mr. Roxbury."

"You are so very kind. I'll await you and your information." He gave her his most winning smile. "And you can be satisfied that you helped reunite a loving man with his beloved wife."

She returned his happy grin. "I'd like that."

With a little waggle of her fingers, the maid continued on her way. Roger watched her go, counting on her believing him and not reasoning through why Hayley left in the first place. *If she informs Rose that I'm seeking Hayley, the game is done.*

Roger waited for nearly a week before the maid sent him a letter. He suspected she was nearly illiterate, for on the envelope was his scrawled address. Inside was a small piece of paper with a barely legible name – Miles Gulch, Wyoming.

"Wyoming," he burst out, surprised. "What is in Wyoming, for heaven's sake?"

Wondering if the maid simply created a bizarre name in a far away territory as a way of earning her bribe, Roger dropped the note on the table. Again, he considered the idea Hayley had gone to her only living relative, her grandmother. If she was even still alive.

Somehow the maid had wheedled the information out of someone. *If* it was true…

Pacing his hallway, Roger thought hard. He tried to remember if Hayley had ever mentioned where her grandmother lived, and what her name was. If she had, he had long forgotten it as unimportant. Now, it was essential he remember.

Even though he had already done it, Roger went up the stairs to Hayley's room. She had left nothing behind to indicate where she had gone. But perhaps a second look might reveal the grandmother's name. Opening the drawers in the bureau, he searched carefully. Nothing. The same in her armoire, and the jewelry box she'd left behind.

Frustrated, Roger sat on the bed, contemplating the huge risk of getting on a train for the distant west on scrawled words of an illiterate housemaid. Yet….

"How many people in Pennsylvania take trains to obscure towns like Miles Gulch?"

Trotting back down the stairs, Roger grabbed his coat and left the house. Using some of his dwindling cash, he hailed a cab. "Train station, please."

At last feeling that he was on Hayley's trail, Roger relaxed as the driver took him the miles to the railway station. Again, he tried to remember Hayley's grandmother's name. Should he go all the way to Wyoming, he'd need the name in order to find both her and Hayley. Yet, if Hayley used her own name out there, the townspeople may have gotten to know her by now.

"Please wait here," he told the driver as the hansom cab stopped at the station.

Diving amid the people coming and going from the trains parked on the rails, Roger ducked into the station. He found the clerk who had assisted him before, ignoring the man's look of resignation and plaintive sigh.

"Can you tell me if any passengers booked a ticket to Miles Gulch, Wyoming?" Roger asked. "It would have been a few weeks ago."

Opening his ledgers, the clerk ran his finger down the lists, turning page after page. Roger waited, containing his urge to dance in impatience, watching the finger slide down the columns.

"Yes, here it is," the clerk said at last. "Miss Marlene Jones bought a ticket to Miles Gulch, Wyoming Territory."

So it's true! "I'd like to buy a ticket to that town," Roger said, growing excited. "How much and when is the next train leaving?"

Consulting a schedule, the clerk replied, "It's leaving at the end of the week, sir."

"Excellent." Roger bought his ticket.

The cab took him back to his townhouse during which Roger contemplated finding Hayley and her grandmother. *It's a small town so tracking her there shouldn't be difficult. When I find her, I'll take the jewels, and get rid of the old woman. If Hayley puts up a fight, I'll get rid of her, too. Or I might make her come back here with me.*

Thinking of having his wife at his beck and call again, Roger started to chuckle, then laughed out loud. "Welcome home, Hayley."

CHAPTER 7

Opening the letter Matt brought from town, Hayley read it with growing incredulity. It was from William and brought both good and bad news. In the weeks since her arrival in Wyoming and Eunice's house, she had started to feel safe at last. Now she wasn't so sure she was safe at all.

"What does it say?" Eunice asked, seated in the warm kitchen with a cup of tea.

"It's from William. He needs me to sign the court's decree dissolving my marriage," Hayley replied, looking at the document that came with William's letter. "Once I send it back, I'll no longer be married to Roger."

Eunice beamed. "That is excellent news, child. I'm so happy for you. Now you can consider accepting Matt's affections."

Hayley flushed. "So you know about that."

"I have eyes, dear. I may be old, but I'm hardly senile. Of course, I know you have grown fond of him. And Jack."

"Yes, that may be true," Hayley admitted. "But I'm not certain I'm ready or that I want anything to go further."

"You couldn't pick a better man than Matt," Eunice went on, stubborn. "Believe me, I know. I have an excellent nose for character. That's how I knew Roger was a bad one. And I know Matt will treat you right, the way you should be treated."

Hayley shook her head, gazing down at William's letter. "William also says that Roger lost his job."

Eunice frowned. "How does your friend know that?"

"William says he's been keeping an eye on Roger," Hayley replied, rereading William's words. "Just in case he finds out where I am. He says to be prepared, as Roger has nothing to keep him in Pennsylvania any longer."

"But how can the man know where you went?"

"I'm praying he can't, Granny. But Roger is smart. I left nothing behind with your name or the name of Miles Gulch on it. Even so, I took Mother's jewels. He thinks of them as his property, and now if he's unemployed, he'll search for me."

"If he's that smart," Eunice declared, "then he should be smart enough not to come here. He'll have to contend with both Matt and me."

Hayley chuckled. "Except he doesn't know about either of you."

"You never told him you have a grandmother?"

"Yes, a long time ago," Hayley answered. "I'm sure he's forgotten, however, as we've never spoken of you since."

"Even so," Eunice went on in her no-nonsense tone, "we'll have to be careful. Matt doesn't need to know anything until after your marriage is legally dissolved."

While Hayley agreed with that statement, her conscience stirred. A lie of omission was still a lie in her opinion. "I know he shouldn't know anything just yet," she said slowly. "But I hate not to be candid with him."

"If you were in a courtship relationship with him, I would agree with you." Eunice stirred her tea. "You should tell him everything. However, you are not in that relationship, at least not yet. Should you enter into such, then you must tell him everything."

"I will."

While Jack had stayed at Eunice's house, healing, Matt spent as much time as possible there. Since he had recovered, he and Matt worked their own ranch in addition to arriving every morning and every evening to feed the stock. Hayley insisted upon learning everything she could so that one day she and Eunice did not need to depend upon them.

Thus, the pair rode in late in the afternoon as Hayley donned sturdy boots acquired in town and joined them in the barn. The weather had cooperated a bit and the sun had melted the snow. Hayley sloshed through the mud as Matt and Jack dismounted at the barn.

"Want me to start teaching you to ride?" Jack asked eagerly.

Hayley glanced at Matt. He returned a half grin and a shrug, indicating without words that it was her choice.

"Don't you both have work at your ranch?" she asked.

"Not for a couple of days," Jack replied, enthusiastic. "We can bring over our old red horse tomorrow."

Reluctant, still not used to life in the country, Hayley hadn't yet gotten very comfortable being around the big animals. Still, she nodded. "I suppose tomorrow will be all right," she said slowly. "Weather permitting."

"Great."

Jack ran to start feeding the corralled horses while Hayley strode next to Matt for the barn. "I confess I'm nervous about riding a horse," she admitted.

"That's natural," he told her, opening the barn door. "But don't let that stop you. There are no cabs out here, and if there's an emergency, you need to be able to ride."

Hayley silently agreed. *Granny is old, I may have to ride to get a doctor.* "I hope I don't fall off."

In the barn, Matt paused to look at her. "That's also part of learning," he said gravely. "If you fall off, you get right back on."

"Why?"

"If you don't, the next time you're faced with riding, you'll remember the fall. And you won't do it."

"Isn't that the same idea of not letting the horse beat you?" she asked, smiling a little.

"True," he replied with a grin. "If you get bucked off, you don't let him win. But a fall is not always from a buck."

"I think I understand what you're saying."

Matt stepped closer and took both of her hands in his. Hayley gazed up into his face, her nervousness rising at the intensity of his expression.

"I really like you, Hayley," he said, his voice low. "I know there's not much to do out here, but I'd like to court you."

Panic nibbled at the edges of her mind. "I – I like you, too," she admitted. "I'm just not certain."

"Of what?"

"What I'm ready for."

"I won't push you," Matt murmured. "But will you let me take you for a ride in the buggy?"

Hesitating, Hayley briefly considered the idea of being away from home with him when she had only known him for a few weeks. *Was that a proper custom out here in the west?* Eunice's words echoed in her mind – Matt was a good man. That encouraged her, and her confidence rose.

"Yes. I'd like that."

Matt grinned. "How about after your lesson? Then Jack can keep Mrs. Parkland company."

"I'm sure she'd enjoy that," Hayley answered, smiling. "She's so very fond of you both."

"The same way we feel about you."

Before she realized his intention, Matt bent and kissed her. Though she felt startled, she didn't pull away from him. His mouth moved sweetly, tenderly over hers, a kiss filled with promise and no demands. Liking his kiss, his nearness, Hayley was disappointed when Matt pulled away.

"Was that okay?" he asked.

"Y-yes," she said, feeling both flustered and safe. She wasn't used to feeling safe when she was alone with a man, and she realized anew just what her life had been with Roger.

He grinned. "Good. I hate getting my face slapped."

Hayley squeezed his fingers, then let his hands go, her own grin now matching his. "I-I feel strange being kissed with all these eyes watching me." She gestured toward the horses and cows eyeing them hungrily.

"Next time, I'll ask them to turn their backs."

Naturally, Eunice insisted Matt and Jack stay to supper. Over the thick beef stew and hot bread, Hayley hardly took her eyes from Matt's. His rugged attractiveness fascinated her, his easy grin and warm gaze made her feel worthy of being loved again. Perhaps in him she might find real love, not the tortured "love" Roger handed out.

Nor will he hurt me.

"Hayley already said yes." Matt's voice broke into her thoughts. "But I hope it's all right with you that I take her for a ride in the buggy, Mrs. Parkland."

"Just wrap her up warm," Eunice replied, doling out more stew onto Jack's plate. "She's a delicate little thing."

"I'm not *that* delicate, Granny," Hayley protested. "Am I not going out every morning and night to feed?"

Eunice sniffed as she eased back into her chair. "You're not as tough as you think, child. You spent all your life indoors with servants to wait on you. Wyoming will make you tough, but you're not there yet."

"I'm going to start teaching her to ride," Jack said, indulging in his second helping of stew. "That'll help make her tough."

"I'm sure it will," Eunice answered. "Especially if she falls off now and then."

"Granny!"

Matt and Jack both laughed while Hayley glowered. "That's not nice to say," Hayley grumbled.

"Nothing teaches faster than a few bruises," Eunice said, her tone bland. "You come off, you learn to get back on. I certainly had my share of falls in my day."

"And what if I get seriously hurt?" Hayley turned her expression on Matt and Jack, both of whom sobered immediately.

"You won't," Eunice replied, unperturbed. "You'll get dirty, but a little dirt won't hurt you."

"Riding a horse doesn't sound like much fun," Hayley commented. "Getting bruised and dirty, yee haw."

Despite her concerns for getting dirty and hurt, Hayley did enjoy her first riding lesson. As Matt sat on the corral fence and Eunice watched from the window, Jack stood in the center of a circle, the red horse at the end of a long rope. Perched uncomfortably atop the red gelding, Hayley was filled with nervousness and anxiety.

"Relax," Matt called as the horse ambled around the circle. "You're too stiff up there. Loosen your shoulders and legs."

Holding onto the saddle horn for her very life, Hayley looked at the ground so very far away.

"Look up," Jack ordered. "You look at the ground, that's where you'll land."

"Deep breaths," Matt yelled. "Breathe in, then out. Relax."

Her head up, Hayley did as he said. Breathing in and out slowly, she worked her shoulders to relax them.

"Sit up straight," Jack said. "Now let Red do the work and practice feeling how he moves."

Hayley obeyed, concentrating on how the horse's muscles worked as he plodded around and around, gazing ahead between his ears. "This isn't so bad," she said at last.

"You're flopping on him like an empty sack," Jack commented critically. "Shoulders up, head up, keep your feet firm in the stirrups."

Hayley sat straighter in the saddle, and instantly felt the balance she had lacked earlier.

"Better," Jack told her. "Now we'll trot."

Before Hayley could stop him, Jack clucked at the horse. Instantly, the gelding broke into a trot. Hayley uttered a tiny shriek, fighting to keep her balance at the hard bouncing. Sliding, she knew she couldn't stay on despite her grip on the saddle horn.

"Whoa," Jack called.

The gelding halted. Still sliding, Hayley dropped from the saddle into the mud at the gelding's feet. Hitting the ground on her backside, she felt her teeth click sharply together. Looking up, she saw the horse's head angling down toward her, his big brown eyes almost sympathetic.

Jack arrived to help her up. "It takes practice," he commented, his hand in hers as he hauled her to her feet. "Let's try again."

Seeing Matt's amusement, Hayley grit her teeth, determined to ride the darn horse. Trying to dust her skirts, she only smeared mud around. "I'll get the saddle dirty," she muttered, reaching up to the saddle horn as Jack gave her a leg up.

"Sit back in the saddle and move with the horse," Jack ordered, then clucked.

The gelding moved forward, and by concentrating, Hayley fought to keep her balance even as the beast trotted. By the lesson's end, she was sore, filthy and happy.

"I did it," she crowed. "I stayed on."

Matt jumped down from the rail and strode to the gelding's side. "You did great," he said, grinning. "And you had your first fall."

"I expect that from your words there will be more?" Hayley asked, her tone arched.

"Yep. Now ease your leg over the cantle, and dismount." His grin widened. "The *proper* way."

Doing as he said, Hayley slid down from the tall gelding, and smiled up at Matt. "Now you have me addicted," she commented. "I want to ride as often as possible."

"So you will," he replied gallantly. "Are you ready to go for our buggy ride?"

"Just as soon as I change out of these filthy clothes. I wouldn't want you to think ill of me if I were to accept this invitation while looking so terrible."

CHAPTER 8

Admiring Hayley's natural beauty, her poise even when covered in muck and mud, Matt handed her up into the small buggy. She had changed into a pale green dress that matched her eyes, a sunbonnet and a thick cloak. He had brought with him a buffalo robe and tucked it around her legs and waist.

"I wouldn't want Mrs. Parkland mad at me for not keeping you warm," he said with a wink.

She laughed lightly, a pleasing and happy sound he liked hearing. "She tends to fuss."

Matt slapped the reins on the black mare's rump, sending her out of the yard at a brisk trot. "You have a beautiful smile. Do you know that?"

"No, I've never been told such."

Matt eyed her sidelong. "Really?"

"Really."

"Then I reckon I'm glad to be the first," Matt told her. "I just hope to be the reason you smile more."

Hayley rested her hand on his. "Be patient with me, Matt. Things have not been easy for me. I can't say more right now."

Glancing at the faint scars etched into the skin of her face, Matt wondered just exactly how rough she'd had it. *Who put those there? A beau? A deceased husband? But if so, why hasn't she spoken of one? What were her real reasons for coming way out here from Pennsylvania?*

But Matt knew he needed to wait on Hayley to tell him in her own time. By her reserved manner up until lately, he suspected she had difficulty in trusting. Not that he blamed her. She'd only known him for a few weeks.

"Where are we going?" Hayley asked.

"There's a little lake a few miles yonder," he replied. "A real pretty spot. I thought you might like to see it."

"That sounds very nice."

"Right now, it's frozen over," he added. "But in summer, it's a great fishing spot. I like to watch the hawks fishing."

"Hawks?" she asked. "As in birds? Fishing?"

"Sure. They circle high over the lake, and when they spot a fish, they dive down and grab it."

"Incredible."

Matt pointed upward at a pair of hawks circling a short distance away. "You know hawks are like people?" he asked. "They mate for life."

"I didn't know that."

"Interesting birds," Matt went on. "Both the male and the female look after and hunt for the babies in the nest."

"What are those?" she asked pointing off to the side.

"Pronghorn antelope," Matt replied, glancing at the tan and white creatures that almost blended in perfectly with the grass around them. "Very good eating."

The trotting horse and the buggy's wheels disturbed a number of birds into flight. They rose from the yellow grass and snow, cheeping in alarm, flying in a flock to quieter regions. Hayley pointed out the snowshoe hares that also fled from their presence.

"What animals are dangerous?" she asked.

"Well," Matt answered slowly. "Most critters will run from you. Even bears and wolves. They're truly dangerous only if you corner them or interfere with their offspring. We have rattlers you have to watch for. Badgers ain't scared of much, not even people, but they won't bother you unless you bother them first."

Hayley gazed out over the prairie. "So much to learn about living here."

"The worst critter to get on the wrong side of are the buffalo." Matt pointed out the herd grazing in the distance. "They're mean and won't hesitate to run you down if you look at them crossways."

"So remind me to never get on the wrong side of one." Hayley smiled in such a fashion that Matt felt his heart melt.

"I promise."

The lake lay in the middle of a shallow valley, and Matt reined the horse in at the top of a gradual hill. He didn't just want Hayley to view the scenery, but to admire the distant Tetons.

"Aren't those grand?" he asked, gesturing. "Almost like the teeth of the world."

"Mountains," Hayley breathed, clearly awed. "I've never seen such mountains before."

"You should see them up close," Matt commented. "Maybe I'll take you there."

"I'd like that. How far away are they?"

"Oh, maybe forty, fifty miles. As wild and untamed as the west itself. I hunt there every summer."

Continuing on down to the lake's edge, Matt reined the mare in again. Jumping down, he assisted Hayley in getting out, then tied the reins to a tree branch. The wind off the ice-covered lake was brisk, but Hayley didn't seem to feel it. Her face reddened slightly from the cold as she stared out over its expanse. Matt took her hand in his, and she turned to him with a smile.

"This is so beautiful," she exclaimed, her hazel eyes bright, happy. "You must think I'm silly, knowing so little about the land and the animals out here."

"Hardly," Matt replied with a grin. "If you took me to the big city, I reckon I'd be as wide eyed and naïve as you are here."

She laughed. "The big city is not nearly as pleasant as this place. But it does have its attractions."

Leading Hayley by the hand, Matt walked with her to the lake's shore. "I don't think I'd care much for the big city," he said. "Too many people. Can't hear yourself think."

"And I feel like the sky here is endless," Hayley answered, gazing up into the cloudless blue. "Look at how open this all is. How beautiful."

Matt pulled her face toward him with his finger under her chin. "Look at this beauty right here," he murmured.

He bent to her and kissed her. As in the barn, Hayley responded with an innocence, a naïveté he liked. Yet, Matt judged she had been kissed before, as she didn't shy away from him. He tasted some experience in the way she kissed him back, in her arms sliding around his neck.

Releasing her, Matt grinned down into her eyes. "Now I could do that all day long."

Hayley giggled. Resting her cheek against his chest, she let him hold her close. "I could do this all day."

"Then I'll just have to free up my schedule to accommodate you, ma'am."

Hayley stiffened in his arms. She raised her head from his chest. "Matt. There are horsemen over there."

Following the direction of her eyes, Matt gazed north. At the valley's rim, a band of riders trotted toward the herd of buffalo. By the way they rode, he instantly recognized them as Cheyenne. "Indians," he said.

Hayley drew away from him yet kept her hand in his. "Are they intending to attack us?"

While her voice sounded calm, Matt felt her fingers trembling. "No," he answered. "That's a hunting party." He gestured toward the slow-moving herd of buffalo.

The band vanished down behind the hills. Matt tested the wind, and guessed the Indians planned to circle behind the herd in order to approach upwind of the unsuspecting buffalo. The herd seemed to notice nothing amiss and continued to graze peacefully. Several long minutes passed.

The Indians didn't reappear. From behind the hills came the sound of sharp pops echoing across the valley. Matt squinted at the herd, observing them begin to move, to stampede. More rifle shots cracked from the hunting Indians.

A jolt of fear raced down Matt's spine. "They're headed right for us."

"Oh, dear God," Hayley breathed.

Half dragging Hayley with him, Matt ran for the horse and buggy. "We have to get out of here. Now."

Untying the mare's reins, Matt grabbed Hayley around her waist and tossed her up onto the seat. He scrambled up behind her, seeing the herd charging straight toward them. Slapping the reins on the mare's rump, Matt turned the horse around to face the road.

"Hiyaaa!" he yelled, urging the mare into a gallop, his hands on the reins encouraging her into a greater speed.

"They're getting closer."

Matt risked a quick glance over his shoulder. The buffalo had reached the lake, their hooves kicking up grass and snow behind them. He saw nothing of the hunters, nor could he hear rifle shots over the thunder of the mare's hooves and the stampeding herd.

The mare raced over the low-lying hills, the buggy bouncing over ruts in the road. Hayley clung desperately to the metal pole that held up the buggy's roof, her hair spilling out from under her bonnet. The leading buffalo flanked the buggy, charging almost alongside.

Fearing the panicked animals might suddenly swerve into them, striking the horse as well as the buggy and trampling all of them, Matt tried to watch the road and the buffalo at the same time. The mare, though not built for speed, stayed just ahead of the stampede.

Hayley uttered a sharp cry as a lead buffalo veered toward them. Matt sucked in his breath, bracing himself for the coming impact, and subsequent crash. In his mind's eye, he briefly envisioned the buggy overturned, the pounding hooves of the pursuing herd crushing both Matt and Hayley as well as the mare underneath them.

At the last second, the buffalo turned away, galloping toward the south. The few leaders to Matt's left also turned southward, following the other. One galloped across the mare's path, forcing her to slow for a brief moment. Risking a glance behind, Matt saw the entire herd shifting direction, charging headlong across the plain.

"All right, that was a little scary," Matt commented, reining in the heavily sweating mare.

"A little scary?" Hayley's voice rose on a squeak. "I'd say that's an understatement."

Pulling the mare down to a walk so she could catch her breath, Matt watched the herd vanish over the plain. "Next time, I suggest we head back the instant we see the Indians."

Matt grinned at Hayley. "Has your heart slowed yet?"

She drew breath to gasp a laugh, her hand pressed to her bosom. "I don't think so. My heavens, you weren't kidding when you said those animals are dangerous."

"Well, cattle are usually docile, but in a stampede like that, even they run in a blind panic."

"The Indians didn't set that herd on us deliberately, did they?" Hayley looked back over her shoulder as though expecting an attack.

"I don't think they even knew we were there," Matt replied. "They needed to launch their hunt upwind while we were downwind. I should have gotten us out of there a tad sooner."

Hayley gathered the robe around her legs. "At least we're safe. Unless they turn and will run back this way."

Matt took her hand while holding the reins with the other. "Not likely. They've probably run their panic off by now. I'm sure the Indians shot what they needed and won't hunt again for a while."

"I can't imagine living the way they do," Hayley commented, gazing south where the buffalo vanished. "Surviving in tents, hunting and killing for food." She plucked at the robe. "Wearing the skins."

"They've been doing it for thousands of years," Matt replied with a shrug. "We aren't much different. We raise our cattle and slaughter them for meat and hides."

Hayley watched his face. "You're right," she admitted slowly. "In the city, we buy our meat at the stores, our leather shoes from a cobbler. I guess I'd never looked at it from the perspective of one who must actually kill to survive."

Matt chuckled. "See? You're turning into a right country girl."

"Perhaps I am." She squeezed his hand, smiling faintly. "But I'm a city girl at heart."

CHAPTER 9

His satchel in hand, Roger stepped off the train into the dismal, muddy and small town of Miles Gulch, Wyoming Territory. Gazing at the lackluster structures, the few people walking, riding or driving along the main street, he shook his head in astonishment.

"Hayley came *here?*" he muttered, hardly able to believe a refined woman of Hayley's background and breeding would venture to such a horrid place. "What if that idiot maid got it wrong?"

Roger crossed the wooden platform amid townspeople who came to greet the train, then stood near the mud street in indecision. Obviously, no cabs operated in this place. Even if he did discover Hayley had come here, how was he to get around?

Observing a wooden sign that said "hotel" in big letters, Roger made that his destination. His shoes squelched in the thick mud as he crossed the street, cursing Hayley with every step. This was her fault for running away, taking with her the valuable jewels that would keep him in whiskey for at least a year if not more.

A passing wagon drawn by a team of huge mules splashed muck over his trousers and coat. Yet, he caught sight of the gun strapped to the driver's hips and stifled the urge to yell invectives. The last thing he needed was to get shot by some trigger-happy yokel. Muttering under his breath, Roger finished the journey and entered the hotel.

"How can I help you?"

Roger set his satchel down at the counter. "I'd like a room, please."

His limited amount of money severely depleted, Roger winced as he handed over the amount the clerk specified. "Do you happen to know a lady by the name of Hayley Roxbury?" he asked as the clerk gave him a room key.

"I'm afraid I haven't heard the name before," the clerk replied.

"She's new in town."

For an answer, he received a half smile and a shrug. "Your room is at the top of the stairs and to the right."

Tired and dispirited, Roger picked up his satchel, and climbed the stairs. The room itself appeared plain and uninviting, the bed narrow. *At least it's a roof out of the cold.* He set his satchel on the floor, then went to the small window to look out at the depressing view of Miles Gulch.

Sitting in a chair, he contemplated his plight. With only a few dollars left to his name, Roger speculated on how to find Hayley if no one knew who she was. For all he knew, the stupid housemaid got the name wrong, and the real Miss Marlene Jones came here from Pennsylvania.

"No," he murmured. "She's here. I don't believe in coincidences."

Slightly cheered with the prospect of getting his hands on the jewels, and thus gaining the revenue he needed, Roger stared into space. *How to find her? If only I remembered the grandmother's name.* Still, the name remained elusive.

Hoping the hotel provided laundry services, Roger changed his trousers, but the coat he wore was the only one he'd brought. Locking his room's door, he went down the stairs and left the hotel. Hayley might be known at the general store, he suspected, for surely, she had needs that brought her into town.

Recrossing the street, his trouser hems dragging in the mud, Roger reached the sidewalk, and tried to scrape some of the mud from his shoes. Disgusted by the sticky mess that clung to his shoes and clothes, he ambled on toward the general store halfway down the block.

A bell chimed overhead as he went in. The proprietors, who appeared to him to be a husband-and-wife team, watched him expectantly as he crossed the store toward them.

"What can we get you?" the man asked.

"Information, if at all possible," Roger replied. "Do you happen to know of a young woman, new to town, named Hayley Roxbury?"

The couple eyed one another. "No, I'm afraid that name isn't familiar," the man replied. "Who is she and why are you looking for her?"

"She's my wife."

While his answer was truthful, Roger instantly knew he made a mistake by saying so. Both sets of eyes narrowed, staring at him, understanding immediately he was also a stranger in town. And if his wife came here, and he was looking for her, then the circumstances couldn't be good.

"Sorry," the man answered. "We haven't seen any strangers. Except you."

"Thanks, anyway."

Roger turned to walk out, and his eyes caught on a display case of various guns. Pausing, he glanced at them, looking them over. He had never fired a gun in his life, yet how else was he to force Hayley to come with him? He looked back at the proprietors.

"How much are these guns?"

The proprietor ambled over to the display case. "Anywhere from five to ten dollars."

He answered Roger's questions agreeably enough, then sold him a revolver and the bullets to go with it. Before he vacated the store, Roger asked, "Is there a place where I might hire a horse and carriage?"

"The livery is down the street." The man pointed. "He hires out horses, but maybe not carriages."

"Thanks."

Tucking the gun into his belt, Roger left the general store. As most men he saw carried weapons, he thought he didn't look too out of place by carrying one. The day had grown colder as he walked down the street toward the livery stable. In his pocket sat a few coins, and only a few bills. If the horse was expensive, he'd have nothing left.

The proprietor looked him up and down. "Do you even know how to ride?"

Offended, Roger snapped, "Will you rent a horse to me or not?"

The man shrugged. "It's your funeral, I reckon. Two bits for a day."

Roger paid him. "Now you saddle it."

The livery stable owner sent his eyes heavenward in a gesture that only made Roger angrier. To avoid conflict, he leaned against the lintel of the big barn, gazing out into the street. A buckboard wagon rolled toward him, a young man, a young blonde woman and a boy sat on the high seat.

All laughed.

Roger gaped, unable to quite believe his own eyes.

The woman was none other than Hayley.

Jealous anger roared through him. How dare she cavort with another man? She was Roger's *wife!* And there she sat, as bold as anything, enjoying the company of a man not her husband.

Watching them as they halted in front of the general store, Roger mentally made his plans.

CHAPTER 10

"Well, hello, Matt. Jack, you're in luck. I have a piece of peppermint candy that needs a boy."

Hayley glanced around the general store, listening as the proprietors hailed Matt and Jack as old friends. She started to gravitate to the bolts of cloth although Eunice had sent her into town with Matt and Jack to obtain more yarn for her knitting. *I adore that shade of gold, maybe I can purchase enough to make a new gown.*

"Hayley, I want you to meet someone."

Thinking to examine the cloth more closely after the introductions, Hayley recrossed the store to Matt's side.

"Miss Hayley Roxbury, these are Sam and Meg Andrews," Matt said, taking her left hand. "Old friends as well as the owners of this establishment."

"How do you do?" Hayley offered to shake by extending her right hand.

However, the husband and his wife stared at Hayley as though she had just grown horns. Neither accepted her proffered hand. Uncomfortable, she lowered it.

"Hayley Roxbury you say?" Sam asked, still staring.

Matt's pleased grin faded. "Yeah. What's wrong?"

"Oh." Sam blinked as though coming to himself. "A man was just here," he said slowly, gazing at Hayley, "looking for you, ma'am. He claimed to be your husband."

Cold terror spread through Hayley. Her mouth suddenly dry, she pulled her hand from Matt's. Her thoughts scattering into a hundred different directions, she tried to still her hands from shaking by clasping them together. *He's found me, he's found me, he's found me –*

"Hayley!"

Hayley jumped, realizing Matt had spoken her name several times. "I – I need to go home, Matt. I – Granny, I need to go."

Whirling, her fear escalating as she realized Roger might know exactly where she lived with Eunice. *He will kill her, he'll kill me, I have to run, I have to go, he'll follow me and not bother her, oh, dear God, how did he find me?*

She made it as far as the door before Matt's hand on her arm halted her. "Hayley, stop," he demanded, forcing her to look up at him. "Your husband?"

Of course, he would be furious. She had fallen in love with Matt while still married to Roger. Now Roger had found her, he'll kill Matt, too. He'll kill Granny, and Jack and Matt and then Hayley herself. "Matt –"

Jack crept to her side and nestled under her arm. The contact broke Hayley's wild thoughts and imaginings. Her throat impossibly tight, she tried to suck breath in, to say anything to explain. "Matt, I'm sorry."

"You're *married?*"

Looking away from his fierce gaze, Hayley saw Sam and Meg watching them, utterly fascinated by the drama unfolding in their store. Embarrassed, she felt blood rush upward to flame her cheeks.

"Take me home," she whispered. "I'll – I'll explain."

Matt yanked open the door. Holding onto Jack like one drowning, she shivered in more than just cold. As Matt swung Jack up to the seat, Hayley took a moment to glance around the town. Of course, she didn't see Roger leering at her from around a corner.

But she knew he was there. She felt his eyes on her.

Matt hoisted her up to the seat, then untied the reins from the hitching post. His grim expression daunted her. Holding her cloak closed tightly at her neck, she recalled her vow to not get involved with anyone until after the problem Roger posed was gone.

Look at me now. In love with a man who now hates me because I didn't tell him everything.

Hayley didn't start explaining until Matt guided the mules to the road toward Eunice's house.

"I'm married," she said, her voice low, "to a beast."

Though she gazed straight ahead, she felt both Matt's and Jack's eyes on her. "He hit you?"

"Nearly every day. I contacted Granny a few months ago, made plans to escape him, come here. A – a friend, back home, is helping me dissolve my marriage. Had – had our affection – for one another taken a little longer to grow, I'd be free to court."

"And now he's here? Why?"

Hayley looked at him for the first time since she discovered Roger had come. "To kill me."

Matt reeled off a string of curses, Hayley flinching at every one of them.

"I know I should have told you," Hayley went on. "I did plan to, once I knew for certain if what we had between us was real."

"But until then, it was none of my business."

Hayley looked out over the empty plains, the patches of snow, at the birds flying low over the waving yellow grass. *It's over before it started. He'll not want to see me again. It's just as well, for I'm taking the horse Granny gave me and riding away from this place.*

"You're right."

Hayley glanced over Jack's head to meet Matt's blue gaze.

"It wasn't any of my business," he went on. "And any man who beats a woman, wife or no, is not a man at all. He gave you those scars?"

Instinctively, her fingers rose to her cheek. "Yes. And others you can't see."

"Then you should be commended for having the guts to leave, to start over. I'm sorry I got angry. I was jealous." Matt shook his head. "Someone got to you before I could."

"I sent the papers back several days ago," Hayley said, her voice low. "I may be free now, but I won't know for certain until I hear from William."

"William?"

Hayley eyed him sidelong. "A friend, married to my best friend, Rose. They helped me to leave Roger."

"Then good for William and Rose," Matt declared. "So any idea on how this husband found you?"

"I have no idea. But he will kill me. He thinks of me as his property and believes my mother's jewels belong to him."

"He sounds like a right ornery fellow. Wait. Jewels? You're hiding jewels?"

"William warned me in a letter to be careful, that Roger lost his job. He said there wasn't anything keeping him in Pennsylvania. Now he's here. He claims my mother's jewels as his own."

"But," Matt added, spitting in disgust, "we know he's here. He can't take us by surprise. If he wants you, he'll have to go through me to do it."

"And me," Jack exclaimed. "I won't let him hurt you, Hayley."

"Thank you both, but I can't allow either of you to risk yourselves. Or Granny. Once I'm home, I'll pack, and be gone in an hour."

"*No.*"

Matt's vehement protest shocked Hayley. "Matt, I have to."

"No, you don't," he growled, scowling darkly. "I love you. I'm not letting some *jackass* from back east take you from me."

"I can't see you get hurt, Matt," Hayley pleaded. "Or Jack. And if anything happened to Granny –"

"Nothing will, I promise." Matt's scowl deepened. "Does Roger know how to handle a gun."

"No."

"Can he ride?"

Hayley laughed but it came out as a snort.

"Then we hunker down at Mrs. Parkland's," Matt went on, the anger in his voice still present. "Let's say he buys a gun, fine. Will he walk all the way out here? In the cold? It'll be dark in an hour. Does he know where you are, exactly at this minute? Let's presume he does. Both Jack and I can hit a target at three hundred yards."

Horrified, Hayley protested, "You talk of killing him!"

"I'm talking self-preservation," Matt snapped, glowering. "It's not what I would choose, but if it comes to it, we'll be ready. We're talking about your life, Hayley. The law in the west says you can kill a man who's trying to kill you."

"B-but…" she stammered. "But, if I leave, there's no need for anyone to get killed."

"And just where will you go?" Matt demanded. "Back home? On a horse, alone? The next town is three days ride from here. What will you do then?"

"F-find a job, m-make a new start."

"You're *making* your new start," he said. "With me. I love you. I'm *not* letting you go."

Feeling defeated, Hayley stared without truly seeing the open country around her. Trapped, she knew what Matt said made sense. Where could she go? Should she leave, she had no idea where the town he mentioned was. What if she left and fell into the hands of outlaws? She'd read they roamed the west in evil packs.

"Look," Matt went on, his voice no longer angry. "I'll throw a scare into him. Chase him off, make it clear that if he pushes, I'll kill him. Then he'll run home."

Hayley shook her head. "You don't understand. Roger is obsessed. He'll pretend you scared him, then come back in the dead of night. He'll need those jewels to continue his lifestyle. And I will *not* give them up. They were my *mother's*."

"You might be surprised." Matt's grin held her attention. "When faced with a man and a rifle, some men realize that even jewels, or wives, aren't worth getting killed over."

CHAPTER 11

Swearing at the horse under him, Roger jerked the reins, forcing the horse's head up. He kicked its ribs, making it jump forward and he almost lost his balance. Staying in the saddle took every bit of effort he possessed.

"Riding isn't as easy as it looks," he grumbled.

A half mile ahead, he observed the wagon that contained Hayley, the man and the boy. Since they left the store so quickly without buying anything, Roger suspected the storekeepers had informed Hayley he was in town and was searching for her. That cost him the element of surprise.

The horse suddenly jigged sideways, almost unseating him. Roger grabbed the saddle horn at the last second before tumbling from the saddle and righted himself. But in retaliation, he hit the horse's neck with his fist.

"Behave," he yelled.

His strike didn't faze the horse at all. It continued to prance, throwing its head up against the right rein he had on its mouth. A rabbit burst across the road nearly under its front hooves, and the horse half reared, trying to spin. Roger stayed on through sheer luck alone.

Forcing the animal back where he wanted it, Roger growled low in his throat, half terrified the horse would throw him, then trample him under its hooves. He knew next to nothing about horses except that they could be incredibly dangerous.

The wagon was now nearly out of his sight. He kicked the horse into a trot. Pulling its head down, it tried to buck. But his hand on the reins and his shoes in its ribs forced it forward. When it settled into a trot, Roger bounced painfully in the saddle.

"I hate riding," he muttered. "And I hate *you.*"

Up ahead, the wagon pulled off at a large farm. Roger reined in, holding back, then urged the horse toward a thicket. He glanced at the sun as it descended toward the west, realizing he dared not get caught out in the open after nightfall. Not only would the cold kill him, the bears or wolves here in the wild would, too.

The thicket's branches scraped his face, neck and hands. Stopping the horse, he slid down. Then leading the animal, he crept forward toward the farm. Parting the stiff branches, he watched the stranger help Hayley and the boy down. The two went into the house.

The cowboy took the mules toward the big barn and started to unharness them. Roger rapidly calculated his chances of knocking the man out or killing him, then kicking in the door to the house. He grinned as he anticipated Hayley's shock in finding his gun pointed at her head.

"So this is your grandmother's house?" he muttered and looked around, seeking cover for himself and his mount. "Nice place."

Leading the horse, he emerged from the thicket, and headed toward the barn where the cowboy was, keeping the shrubbery between himself and the house. The cowboy had gone inside with the mules. *Perfect.* Pulling his gun from his belt, he held it in his right hand while he kept the reins firmly in his left.

Darkness crept in as Roger neared the barn. He tied the horse to a branch, then, keeping a wary eye on the house, he slipped around to the front. Inside the barn, he heard cows lowing, and the rustling of legs in straw. At the house, lamps were lit against the coming darkness.

His gun in his hand, Roger sneaked a peek around the open barn door. The cowboy's back was to him as he stood beside a cow. Roger grinned. *This is too easy.*

Making as little noise as possible, he sidled slowly up behind the man, his entire attention focused on his prey.

A cat's sudden screech startled him.

The cowboy whipped around, saw him. He lunged forward, reaching for the gun at his hip. Roger, stunned at the man's speed, pulled the trigger reflexively without truly aiming the weapon. His lucky shot struck the cowboy before he had a chance to yank his own gun free.

The cowboy stumbled, then fell to the straw.

Panting, not quite understanding exactly what happened, Roger stared at the form at his feet. At the sound of the shot, the animals in the barn spooked, spinning in their stalls.

Roger knew the gunshot would have been heard by those in the house.

He had to move fast.

Leaving the barn, he trotted toward the house, then stopped. "Hayley!" he yelled. "I killed your beau. Come out now, or I'll come in there and kill you all."

CHAPTER 12

Eunice listened with a strange calm as Hayley explained that Roger had found her. "He was at the general store, asking for me."

"I reckon that was to be expected," Eunice replied, rising stiffly from her chair. "Jack, son, it's getting dark. Light the lamps, please."

Jack scurried to obey. Astonished that Eunice's reaction was not at all what she expected, Hayley rushed on. "He may come here, Granny. I can't risk you or Jack or even Matt getting hurt."

Eunice patted Hayley's cheek as she passed. "Don't you worry, child. That boy will be in a world of hurt if he comes here."

"But, Granny."

Her words fell on deaf ears. Eunice, leaning on her stick, made her slow way into her room. The house burned with light as Hayley peered through the curtains out into the yard.

Nothing moved. Matt would be in the barn caring for the stock. Hayley wished he was here in the house.

She didn't like them being separated.

A gunshot made her jump.

"Oh, no!"

Hayley ran for the door. Yet, before her hand reached for the knob, Eunice's sharp voice cracked from behind her.

"Don't open that door!"

Hayley whirled.

Eunice, striding more firmly than ever, approached a window. "I reckon he found us."

"Granny!"

Then Roger's shout captured her attention, and she peered through the window.

Hayley! I killed your beau. Come out now, or I'll come in there and kill you all.

Jack screamed and bolted for the door. Hayley caught him, forced him back even as Eunice strode toward them. Her heart breaking in her breast, Hayley craved to echo his scream, the terrible grief ripping her heart into shreds. *Matt's dead!*

"*Jack,*" Eunice bellowed. "Don't move. We'll deal with him."

"He killed Matt," Jack howled, sobbing.

"Just you settle down, youngster," Eunice ordered. "Sit there."

Unable to believe Jack did as she commanded, Hayley stared out at Roger in the middle of the yard, her grief swamping her.

"Hayley," he shouted again. "Come here. If you come out peacefully, I won't kill anyone else."

Hayley spun on Eunice, her throat choking her. "I have to go."

"No, you will not."

"I have to. I can't let him hurt you."

"Hayley!" Roger roared.

Spinning, Hayley charged out the door. "I'm coming, Roger. Don't shoot."

Even as Eunice yelled for her to come back, Hayley, knowing she walked to her death, continued forward. Her eyes on Roger, she didn't want to live with the knowledge she got Matt killed. This was her fault, and she would pay the price with her life.

Roger grinned malevolently. "Hello, Hayley. I've missed you so."

"You have me, Roger. Just have done with it. Kill me. And spare the lives of those in the house."

Roger's hand smacked her hard across the cheek. Though she expected it, Hayley's head snapped painfully on her neck. She faced him again, finding a courage she didn't know she had to look him in the eye.

"Are you happy now?" she sneered. "Big man hitting a woman weaker than he is?"

"You forgot something, my darling," Roger growled, seizing her by her upper arm. "I want those jewels. You'll march back in there, and if you're not here in thirty seconds with them, I'll kill everyone in there, including you."

Working saliva into her dry mouth, Hayley spat in his face.

His countenance dark with rage, Roger slammed his fist into her cheek, knocking her to the ground. "How dare you," he snarled, standing over her with the gun in his hand. "How –"

A gunshot split the dusk's quiet.

Roger shrieked in agony, dropped his gun and clutched his arm. Dazed, Hayley craned her head, seeing Matt leaning against the barn door, aiming his gun for another shot.

Roger also saw him. He bent and seized the gun.

He bolted across the yard, running hard, and Matt's next shot missed. Hayley rolled to her feet, intending to run to Matt. Clearly, he was hurt, but oh so very much alive. Even as Roger vanished into the shadows near the barn, Hayley charged across the yard to Matt.

"Matt," she gasped. "How bad?"

"My shoulder. I'll be all right. Where'd he go?"

"I don't –"

A crashing from the underbrush heralded a horse and rider. Roger charged into the open, in the saddle, but hardly in control of the animal he rode. He raised his pistol, aiming it at Hayley even as the horse slid to a trampling halt.

Hayley cried out.

She shoved Matt back into the barn, throwing herself out of the way of the bullet. It fired.

The bullet plowed into the barn's wall well over Hayley's and Matt's heads. Outside, the horse's hooves stamped on the ground, Hayley heard Roger shriek in fear. Peering around the wall, she watched as Roger fought to control his now out-of-control mount.

The horse spun in circles, foam covering its muzzle, its eyes showing the white. Unable to halt the mad beast, Roger jerked hard on the reins. He dropped the gun as he seized a hold of the saddle horn. But his hard grip on the bit only maddened the horse more.

Unable to move forward with Roger's hard grip on the reins, the horse reared. Its front hooves boxing the dusk, Hayley saw its head and flowing mane outlined against the stars in the sky. Higher and higher, the horse seemed to leap into the air –

It reared too high.

Overbalanced, it fought to remain on its rear legs. Roger's heavy hand on the reins pulled the animal over backwards. He screamed, once, as the horse crashed onto its back, its full weight landing on him, crushing him beneath its body.

Unable to move, Hayley stared. The horse scrambled to its feet, then galloped into the near darkness. She listened to its fading hoofbeats as she slowly walked toward the still form on the ground. Behind, Matt grunted, following her, his breath hissing through his teeth in pain.

The front door slammed.

Jack screeched as he ran across the yard and threw his arms around Matt's waist. "You're alive."

"Yeah, son, I'll be all right."

Hardly aware of Eunice arriving, Hayley gazed down at Roger. There was nothing that could be done. Even in the near darkness, she saw the damage done to his body. His chest had crushed under the impact of horse and saddle. He bled from his nose and mouth, his pleading eyes on hers.

Kneeling beside him, Hayley took his cold hand. He was her husband, after all.

"Good-bye, Roger," she whispered. "Die in peace."

He tried to speak. Instead, blood gushed from his mouth and nose. Then he was gone. Just like that.

Hayley bowed her head. Yet, no tears burned her eyes, or stung her nose. He had brought this on himself. He abused her for years with his cruelty, then followed her across the country in order to kill her. She never wanted this, nor did she ask for him to be as brutal and obsessive as he was.

A strong hand under her arm lifted her to her feet. Hayley buried her face in Matt's uninjured shoulder, hiding the sight of her dead husband by closing her eyes.

"Let's go into the house," he said softly.

EPILOGUE

Hayley paid for Roger's funeral out of the money she had taken from their bank account. Though Eunice refused to attend, and wouldn't allow Jack to go, either, Hayley stood hand in hand with Matt as the preacher intoned prayers for the dead.

They were the only two mourners.

"I loved him once," she said softly. "A long time ago."

"I know."

Matt's free arm, the one not in the sling, draped across her shoulders, and pulled her close. "We can't see the future," he murmured. "We always wish we could, but we can't."

"I know."

"This wasn't your fault."

Hayley gazed up into his impossibly blue eyes. "I know that, too."

"I love you."

"I love you, too. I want to spend the rest of my life with you."

"Then I hope you'll marry me."

Somehow, it didn't surprise her that she received a marriage proposal at her ex-husband's funeral. For William had wired the information that she was free from her marriage to Roger. And that due to his death, she inherited the townhouse.

William would arrange the sale in her name and wire the funds to her.

Hayley smiled up into his face. "You know I will marry you."

"Good."

The preacher spread dirt upon the grave even as Hayley and Matt turned to walk away.

Hayley leaned into Matt. "When I marry you, I will have an instant family. A son and a husband. I like it."

"And we'll have more children," Matt said and kissed her forehead. "Many more children."

The End

CONTINUE READING...

Thank you for reading *The Pretend Mail Order Bride!* Are you wondering **what to read next?** Why not read *Escaping Her Fiancé's Rumors?* **Here's a peek for you:**

Justine stared at him, disbelieving. "You're *what?*"

"Don't play games," Percy replied, his voice tense, his face taut. "You heard me clearly enough. I'm not going to marry you, and that's that. I do hope you'll maintain your dignity and not cry all over the place."

That remark, delivered with cold cruelty, slapped against Justine. She did her best to stifle the tears that were so close to falling. "I-I certainly would not wish to cause you embarrassment," she said, shocked that her voice even worked.

I love him, he said he loved me. What happened to all that?

Percy lifted his upper lip in a doglike sneer. "I'm worth crying over, my dear, as you'll see. However, it's you who is not worthy of my attention or my wedding ring."

"But you said… I was certainly worthy when we –" Justine swallowed the words. "What you begged me to do."

"And that is exactly why you no longer interest me." Percy gazed down his long nose at her, and something in Justine snapped, and suddenly, she came very close to slapping him across his face. "You're a light skirt, Justine. I cannot respect, or marry, a loose woman."

Shame brought a flush to her cheeks. Hardening her voice, Justine asked, "So that's all you were after? You never loved me? Never truly wanted to marry me? You pressured me and deceived me, and now just toss me aside like yesterday's newspaper?"

"No one will marry you, my dear." Percy smiled as though that had been his intention all along. To use her, then make certain no other man would consent to make her his wife. "The news has already spread across half of Boston. Haven't you noticed the stares? The sniggers?"

"I-I've heard nothing," Justine stammered, shaking with shame and humiliation, "I haven't. But they're your friends, not mine."

"Word is spreading," Percy went on with a shrug, still smiling. "Soon you will not be able to show your face in public."

"But why would you do this, Percy?" Justine asked, blinking back her tears. "What have I done to make you so hateful? You used to be kind."

"That doesn't matter." A shield came down over his eyes, hiding whatever might lie behind them. "Go. Leave my house, and don't ever come back."

Visit HERE To Read More!

https://ticahousepublishing.com/mail-order-brides.html

Susannah has always been intrigued with the Western movement - prairie days, mail-order brides, the gold rush, frontier life! As a writer, she's excited to combine her love of story with her love of all that is Western. Presently, Susannah lives in Wyoming with her hubby and their three amazing children.

www.ticahousepublishing.com
contact@ticahousepublishing.com